Dracula
Doesn't Drink
Lemonade

layton

There are more books about the Bailey School Kids!
Have you read these adventures?

Dracula Doesn't Drink Lemonade

by **Debbie Dadey**
and
Marcia Thornton Jones

illustrated by John Steven Gurney

A
LITTLE APPLE
PAPERBACK

SCHOLASTIC INC.
New York   Toronto   London   Auckland   Sydney

For Myra and David Rosenfeld — MTJ

For Diane, John, Cori, Nicki, and
Stefan Vallentine — DD

No part of this publication may be reproduced in whole or in part, or
stored in a retrieval system, or transmitted in any form or by any means,
electronic, mechanical, photocopying, recording, or otherwise, without
written permission of the publisher. For information regarding
permission, write to Scholastic Inc., 555 Broadway,
New York, NY 10012.

ISBN 0-590-22638-X

Text copyright © 1995 by Marcia Thornton Jones and Debra S. Dadey.
Illustrations copyright © 1995 by Scholastic Inc.
All rights reserved. Published by Scholastic Inc.
APPLE PAPERBACKS is a registered trademark of Scholastic Inc.

12 11 10 9 8   6 7 8 9/9 0/0

Printed in the U.S.A.   40

First Scholastic printing, October 1995

Book design by Laurie Williams

Contents

1

The Fight

"Stop them!" Liza screamed and pointed to the fighting boys.

Eddie shrugged. "It's only Huey and Ben."

Eddie, Liza, Howie, and Melody were walking into the Bailey Elementary schoolyard. Kids in their third-grade class usually did not fight around school. They were afraid of Mrs. Jeepers, their teacher. Some of the kids even thought she was a vampire. But not Ben. He was in the fourth grade and wasn't afraid of anything. Ben was busy punching Huey's arm.

"We have to stop them," Liza cried. "Ben is older than Huey."

Eddie rolled his eyes. "Why should I help Huey? I don't even like him."

Melody looked at the fighting boys. "Well if you don't stop them, then I guess I'll have to. Ben's bigger than Huey. It's not fair."

"Life is not fair," Eddie told her, but he grabbed Ben by the arm and pulled him away from Huey.

"What's the big idea?" Ben yelled.

Liza jumped in front of Ben and pointed her finger in front of his nose. "You ought to leave third-graders alone, you big meanie."

Ben looked down at Liza and laughed. "Then I'll punch you instead of Huey."

Liza's lip quivered and she looked ready to cry.

"You touch Liza and you'll have to fight me, too," Melody said, pushing Liza aside to stand in front of Ben.

"Me, too," Eddie and Howie both said at the same time. They stood beside Melody and glared at Ben.

Ben laughed again. "I'm not afraid of you pipsqueaks." To prove it, he gave Eddie a push. Eddie shoved back, so Ben pushed him again.

Howie tried to grab Ben's arm to make him stop, but he ended up grabbing Eddie instead. The two of them crashed into the fourth-grade bully. Ben stumbled backwards and fell smack dab into a strange man.

The stranger's dark clothes blended with the shadows of the school building. His pants were black and his long leather coat nearly touched the tops of pointy black cowboy boots. But next to the stranger's slicked-back black hair, his face looked pale, like brittle old bones.

Liza, Melody, Howie, Eddie, and Huey took a giant step backwards as the stranger helped Ben off the ground. "Fighting is not good," the man said softly. His voice was a hoarse whisper, and he talked with a strange accent.

"The fight was all his fault," Ben said.

"Was not," Huey argued. "Ben started it!"

The stranger sighed, shaking his head. "Perhaps you were both at fault," he said in his whispery accent. Then he leaned down so his face was very close to Ben and Huey. He looked deeply into the eyes of both boys before saying, "Fighting is not good. I do not want to see you fighting ever again!"

"Y . . . yes, sir," Huey stammered, backing farther away from the pale stranger.

But Ben just shrugged. "Huey's not worth getting in trouble for," he admitted. Then he turned and walked away, leaving the five kids staring at the man dressed in black.

The stranger smiled, showing crooked pointy teeth. "I am glad that is settled," he said softly. But his smile faded when the early morning sun peeked through the trees and freckled the sidewalk with dancing sunspots. The stranger stepped back into the shadows and frowned. "It is getting late," he warned the kids. "I must go. Quickly!" Without another word, the man stalked away, staying within the shadows.

2

Dead Head

"Where did that man come from?" Eddie asked.

"I don't know," Howie said. "I've never seen him before."

"I've never seen anyone so pale. I bet he never gets in the sun," Liza whispered. "He looks like a ghost."

"Maybe he is a ghost," Eddie said in his scariest whisper.

Melody giggled. "Maybe he's Mrs. Jeepers' long lost vampire husband. His accent is like hers."

"He can't be," Liza told her. "Mrs. Jeepers' husband is dead."

Eddie laughed. "Well, that stranger certainly looked dead to me!"

"That's not funny." Liza shivered, hugging her schoolbooks tightly.

"Liza's right," Howie interrupted. "This is no laughing matter."

"Don't tell me you're a scaredy cat like Liza," Eddie teased.

Howie shook his head. "I mean, it's not funny that Mr. Dead Head just walked into Bailey Elementary!"

"Oh no!" Huey cried. "We better hurry before it's too late."

"Before what's too late?" Melody asked, grabbing his arm before he raced away.

"Before the dead head tells Principal Davis we were fighting," Huey told her.

"Huey's right," Howie said. "If Principal Davis finds out we were anywhere near a fight, we'll all be in big trouble. Let's go!"

The five kids raced up the steps of Bailey Elementary School, scooted in the door, and hurried to Principal Davis' office. They skidded to a stop just outside his door.

"Maybe if we apologize, the stranger won't tell on us," Huey whined.

"I think we're too late," Eddie said. But he forgot to whisper, and his voice echoed down the empty hallway.

Principal Davis turned to face the kids. "Come in," he said. "There's someone I'd like you to meet."

Liza, Melody, Howie, Eddie, and Huey took tiny steps until they were just inside the office door.

"This is Mr. Drake," their bald-headed principal told them. "He is Bailey School's new guidance counselor. I suspect he'll be talking with you quite a bit."

"Guidance counselor?" Eddie asked. "What's that?"

Liza shook Mr. Drake's hand, ignoring Eddie. "Pleased to meet you," Liza said. "My mother said we really need a counselor."

"But what is a counselor?" Eddie asked again.

"He's here to help us solve our problems," Melody told Eddie.

"Problems?" Eddie said. "What problems?"

"Problems like fighting, for instance," Mr. Drake said softly.

Huey and Eddie turned bright red, but Principal Davis didn't seem to notice. "Hurry along," he said when the bell rang. "I wouldn't want you to be late for class."

The five kids walked quickly toward their classroom. "Why don't we ever get any normal teachers around this school?" Eddie complained.

"I'm sure Mr. Drake is nice once you get to know him," Melody said.

Huey shook his head. "That Mr. Drake is strange. He gives me the creeps. Nothing can make me tell him my troubles."

"Don't be silly," Melody said. "People can't help how they look."

"Can they help how they feel?" Liza asked softly.

Howie looked at Liza. "What are you talking about?"

"When I shook Mr. Drake's hand it was as cold as an icicle," Liza whispered nervously. "Cold enough to be dead."

3

New Counselor

The five kids didn't spend any more time talking about icicles or the new counselor. Mrs. Jeepers had nearly covered the blackboard with addition and subtraction problems. They headed straight to their seats and got to work.

Mrs. Jeepers had a way of keeping everybody busy. If someone even thought about stirring up trouble, the teacher flashed her green eyes in that direction. Then Mrs. Jeepers would gently rub the green brooch she always wore. Some kids thought her pin was magic. Others were afraid their teacher was a vampire. Either way, they decided they didn't want to get her mad, so they made it a habit to behave.

The kids worked so hard, they forgot about the new counselor until they saw him on their way to lunch. "He sure is creepy," Melody whispered as the class walked into the cafeteria. "I know he can't help it, but his skin is so pale."

Liza nodded. "I can't get over how cold his hand felt."

The kids followed Mr. Drake into the cafeteria and waited while he eyed the lunch selections. Eddie's stomach growled, reminding him how hungry he was. "The pizza's really good," Eddie blurted out.

Mr. Drake sighed. "Eating big meals in the middle of the day makes my stomach feel like a cave full of nervous bats."

"Everybody gets hungry at lunchtime," Melody said.

Mr. Drake shrugged. "My appetite doesn't really kick in until after the sun goes down. I really enjoy midnight snacks the best!"

"But you should eat something," Liza told him. "You look like you're getting sick."

"If you're not feeling well," Howie added, "you should get some rest and drink plenty of fluids."

"Yes," Mr. Drake said with a tiny smile. "Something to drink would be nice. It seems like I am always thirsty."

Mrs. Tilly smiled from behind the lunch counter and pointed to the end of the line. "There's plenty of milk. Help yourself."

Mr. Drake's face puckered into a frown. "I don't care for milk."

"How about a cold glass of iced tea?" Mrs. Tilly asked.

"I'm afraid I don't like iced tea, either," Mr. Drake moaned.

"Coffee?"

"Definitely not!" Mr. Drake said.

Mrs. Tilly didn't look happy anymore and several kids in the line were grumbling. Everybody was tired of waiting.

"Unless you like lemonade, you'll have to settle for water," Mrs. Tilly said.

"Lemonade?" Mr. Drake asked. "I like lemonade, especially pink lemonade."

"Then you're in luck," Mrs. Tilly said. She poured Mr. Drake a tall glass of pink lemonade and dropped a straw into it.

Mr. Drake picked up the glass and sucked hard on the straw, making slurping noises as he drained the pink lemonade. "Ah," Mr. Drake said, turning to the waiting students. "That hit the spot!"

Then he smiled so big that Howie, Melody, Liza, and Eddie couldn't help noticing his pointy teeth.

4

Dungeon

"Did you see his teeth?" Liza squealed. "They were pointed."

Melody shrugged and pushed back a black braid. "Maybe his parents couldn't afford to get him braces when he was little."

Howie sat down under the oak tree. It was after school and they were at their favorite meeting place. "Crooked teeth are normal," Howie said, "but those teeth didn't look normal to me."

"The only thing normal about this school is us," Eddie said.

Liza giggled and looked at Eddie. "If you're normal, then we're all in trouble."

"I think we *are* in trouble," Howie said. He pointed toward Mr. Davis, their principal. He was heading right for them, and his bald head was beet red.

"He looks mad," Melody said.

"Eddie and Howie!" Mr. Davis yelled. "Come here."

"Uh-oh," Liza whispered. "I bet he found out about this morning's fight."

Howie gulped and ran toward Principal Davis. Eddie shrugged his shoulders before following his friend.

"Boys, I'm in a rush," Mr. Davis told them, "but I want you to stop by Mr. Drake's office before you leave today. He asked to see you two."

Howie swallowed hard and squeaked. "He asked to see us?"

Principal Davis pointed to the school. "He's using the nurse's office. I've got a meeting across town. Be nice now." With a wave, their principal hurried toward his car.

"I'd rather meet with Godzilla than Mr. Drake," Eddie told Howie.

Howie didn't say anything. He nodded

and walked into the school. Both boys stopped before going into the nurse's office. The door was open, but inside, the office was pitch-black.

"It looks like a dungeon in there," Howie whispered.

"It looks like Mr. Drakey-poo forgot about seeing us and went home," Eddie said out loud.

"Eddie? Howie?" a voice called from inside the dark room. "Is that you? Come in."

"I guess we weren't that lucky," Howie said softly.

Howie and Eddie walked into the nurse's office. Usually the office was full of light, but today there was black paper over the windows and the lights were off. The only light came from the open door. Mr. Drake sat in the darkest corner of the tiny room.

"It's awfully dark," Eddie said, reaching for the switch. "Why don't I turn on the lights?"

"No!" Mr. Drake shouted. "Leave the lights off!"

Eddie and Howie both jumped, and Mr. Drake stood up from his chair to apologize. "Excuse me for raising my voice. Bright lights bother my eyes."

"Maybe you should get sunglasses," Eddie suggested.

Mr. Drake laughed. "Perhaps you are right."

"Did you want to talk to us?" Howie asked.

"Yes, thank you for coming," Mr. Drake said. "Please tell me about the fight this morning."

"I'll tell you," Eddie said quickly. "We were just trying to help Huey before Ben knocked a hole in his head."

Mr. Drake put a hand on each boy's shoulder and laughed, showing his pointed teeth. "Holes in the head can be

a real pain in the neck. It was kind of you boys to help Huey. I will certainly be talking with Ben."

Eddie and Howie scooted out of the office and rushed outside the building before stopping. "Yikes!" Eddie said, leaning up against the school building. "Liza was right! Mr. Drake's hands are so cold, he feels dead!"

5

Shadow

A long shadow fell across the two boys. Howie ducked and Eddie whirled around just as Melody and Liza sneaked around the corner of Bailey Elementary.

"What's the matter with you?" Melody giggled. "You're scared of your own shadow."

"It wasn't *our* shadow," Eddie muttered. "You sneaked up on us."

"No, we didn't," Liza told him. "We just came to see if you survived your meeting with Counselor Drake."

Eddie and Howie looked at each other. Neither boy said a word.

"What's wrong? Did the sickly Counselor Drake bite your tongue off with his pointy teeth?" Melody giggled.

But Eddie and Howie weren't laughing.

"He must have really let you have it," Liza said, her eyes wide.

"We're not in trouble," Eddie snapped.

"Then why are you acting like you just lost a pint of blood?" Melody asked.

Howie grabbed Melody's arm. "That's it!"

"What?" Howie's three friends asked at once.

"I just figured out who our new counselor is."

"What are you talking about?" Melody asked. "We already know who he is."

"Do we?" Howie whispered. "You have to admit, the new school counselor seemed to appear out of nowhere."

"So?" Liza said. "New teachers are always showing up suddenly around Bailey School."

"But teachers aren't usually afraid of lights," Howie pointed out. "And their skin isn't white like chalk dust."

"Mrs. Jeepers' is," Liza said softly. "Her skin is very pale, too."

"Exactly!" Howie shouted. "Now you see what I'm talking about."

Melody shook her head so hard her braids thumped against her cheeks. "I don't see anything."

"Mr. Drake isn't a regular school counselor," Howie said slowly. "I don't think he's a counselor at all."

"Then what is he?" Eddie asked.

Howie didn't have a chance to answer

because just then the door to Bailey Elementary School swung open and Mr. Drake peeked outside. He squinted at the sun, not even noticing the four kids huddled by the back door. Mr. Drake threw his long black coat over his shoulders. His collar stuck up, covering his face so only his eyes showed. Then the new counselor glided out of the building and hurried down the sidewalk, keeping to the shadows the entire way.

Howie broke his friends' silence. "Our new counselor," he said very slowly, "is Count Dracula!"

6

C. D.

Eddie fell back against the school building and laughed. "You think Mr. Drake is what?"

"Dracula," Howie said without smiling.

"Howie, you're supposed to be smart," Melody said. "Don't you know that Dracula is just in movies and books?"

Liza put her hand on Melody's shoulder. "It does all sort of fit together."

"This isn't a puzzle," Eddie snickered.

Liza ignored Eddie. "He does have pointed teeth and wears black."

"He's afraid of light," Howie added.

Liza jumped up and down. "Counselor Drake—C. D.!"

"So what?" Eddie said.

Liza rolled her eyes. "Don't you get it?

C. D. stands for Count Dracula!"

"You guys are nuts, completely wal-nuts!" Eddie said, slapping his forehead with his hand.

"There's one way we could find out," Howie said softly. "We could follow him to see where he goes."

"No problem," Eddie said. "Let's go."

"We better not," Liza said. "It could be dangerous."

Melody took off after Counselor Drake. "There's nothing dangerous about a school counselor. Besides, it'll only take a few minutes."

The four kids ran to catch up with Mr. Drake. The counselor drifted from shadow to shadow, his dark clothes blending so well he was hard to see. But they did see when he turned into the old Clancy Estate. Some people said the huge house was haunted. And it was where Mrs. Jeepers lived.

Howie pulled Eddie and Melody into a clump of bushes. Liza hopped in beside them.

"Why are you hiding?" Melody asked.

"Shhh," Howie warned. "Do you want him to hear us?"

"Why would the new counselor be going to Mrs. Jeepers' house?" Liza asked.

"Maybe they have a date," Eddie giggled.

"I don't think so," Howie said slowly. "Look."

"Oh, no!" Liza squealed. "He's going into Mrs. Jeepers' house."

Howie's eyes grew big and he nodded. "Not just her house . . . her basement. And we all know what's in her basement."

Liza gulped. When Mrs. Jeepers moved in, Eddie and Melody saw the movers carry a long wooden box shaped like a coffin into Mrs. Jeepers' basement. They told their friends they heard sounds coming from inside the box.

"I'm scared," Liza whimpered. "Maybe he really *is* Count Dracula."

7

The Mightiest Vampire of Them All

"Mr. Drake is not a vampire," Eddie said. "And he certainly isn't Count Dracula!"

Eddie, Howie, Melody, and Liza stood under their favorite oak tree before school started the next morning. It was a warm morning, and Eddie tossed his jacket to the ground. But Howie kept his jacket zipped all the way up to his chin and a bright red wool scarf wound tightly around his neck.

"But he's sleeping in Mrs. Jeepers' basement," Howie reminded them.

"At least he's sleeping," Melody said softly. "You look like you tossed and turned all night."

It was true. Howie's eyes were underlined with purple circles, and he kept yawning. "Somebody had to stay awake to figure out a plan to save Bailey City," Howie snapped, pulling his red scarf tighter around his neck.

"Save Bailey City from what?" Eddie asked. "From getting strangled by that silly scarf of yours?"

"This is serious," Howie told his friends. "Count Dracula is the mightiest vampire of them all. What are we going to do?"

"We're going to lock you up in the loony bin," Melody said. "That's what!"

"You do seem awfully upset," Liza said softly. "Maybe you should talk to someone. The nurse might help."

"Or the school counselor!" Eddie blurted.

The color drained from Howie's face as if someone had just sucked all his blood. "Are you crazy? I wouldn't go to his office again for all the gold in Fort Knox. It's too dangerous." Howie tugged the scarf tighter around his throat. "We're all in danger . . . grave danger."

Eddie laughed so hard he had to lean back against the rough bark of the oak tree to keep from falling down.

"You won't be laughing when Count Dracula nibbles your neck while you sleep," Howie warned. "At least I plan to be safe."

"For all you know, he's a sickly cousin of Mrs. Jeepers," Melody argued. "After all, who ever heard of a vampire breaking up fights?"

"And I'm sure Count Dracula doesn't drink pink lemonade," Eddie added.

Liza reached out and gently tapped Howie's arm. "Melody and Eddie must be right. Mr. Drake hasn't actually done anything. Maybe it was all our imaginations."

"But you believed me yesterday," Howie gasped. "You felt how cold his hand was. You saw his pale skin."

"And we all recognize your perfectly crazy brain," Eddie interrupted. "Liza's right. We were just imagining things. Let's get to class and forget this Dracula business."

In their classroom they all slid into their seats, ready to start the day. But Howie refused to remove his scarf, even when Mrs. Jeepers gave him her famous glare.

They were working on a reading assignment when there was a knock at the door. Half the class heard Howie gasp when Mr. Drake stuck his head inside the classroom. The new counselor smoothed his ink-black hair back from his pale forehead and smiled, showing his pointy eyeteeth.

"May I have a word with Huey?" Mr. Drake asked Mrs. Jeepers in his strange accent. "It should not take but a moment."

Mrs. Jeepers nodded. "But of course."

"Do you think he's in trouble?" Melody asked as Huey went into the hall.

Howie nodded. "Big trouble."

"Aw, Mr. Drake just wants to ask him about the fight," Eddie said. But then Mrs. Jeepers flashed her green eyes, and the kids quickly got back to work.

Huey was gone for longer than a moment. He didn't come back in a few minutes either. Howie watched the big hand of the clock tick away twenty minutes. By then, it was time for lunch. Huey joined the class as they went into the cafeteria.

The big third-grader sniffed loudly and his face was as white as the cafeteria's mashed potatoes. "Are you okay?" Howie asked.

Huey just stared straight ahead.

"Did you get in trouble?" Liza asked.

Huey still didn't answer. Instead, he took his tray and sat in the corner, far away from the rest of his friends.

Eddie, Howie, Liza, and Melody sat down at their usual table without a word. Howie pushed the peas around on his tray. Finally, he told his friends, "We have to do something about Mr. Drake."

"We don't have to do anything," Eddie said.

Melody nodded. "You can't prove he's Dracula."

Howie pulled his scarf up close to his chin before answering. "Didn't you see how pale Huey was? He was sniffling. Maybe Mr. Drake bit him on the neck."

"That would sure make me cry," Melody giggled.

"You don't know he was crying," Eddie argued. "Maybe he's allergic to brainless idiots wearing wool scarves."

"Huey does have allergies," Liza said. "But I think just to animal fur."

"Animals?" Howie asked. "Like bats?"

Liza's eyes got big, and she pushed her tray away. "You're scaring me, Howie.

Do you really think Mr. Drake bit Huey on the neck?"

"What if he did?" Eddie interrupted. "Who cares about Huey anyway?"

"You should," Howie warned and smacked his hand onto the table. "Everyone knows that once you're bitten by a vampire, you become one, too. And you know Huey's appetite. It won't be long before he's turned us all into vampires." Howie smacked his hand onto the table again. This time his hand hit his fork, sending peas flying into his hair.

"You should see yourself," Liza giggled. "You look crazy."

Eddie snickered. "You should look in a mirror."

"A mirror!" Howie gasped. "That's it. I know exactly how to prove Mr. Drake is a vampire."

8

Reflection

"What's a mirror got to do with anything?" Melody asked.

"He wants to break it, so he'll have seven years of bad luck," Eddie said.

Howie pulled the peas off his head one by one. "If I only had a mirror, I could prove that Mr. Drake is Dracula."

"How?" Liza asked.

"Because," Howie said, "vampires don't have a reflection. They can't show up in a mirror."

Eddie pointed his fork at Howie. "That's right," Eddie said. "I saw it on *Land of the Dead*. It was a great movie. The hero used a mirror to prove who was a vampire."

Howie wiped his ear with a paper napkin. "If only I had a . . ."

"I have one," Liza said softly. She pulled a small pink mirror out of her jeans' pocket and handed it to Howie.

"Why do you have a mirror?" Melody asked.

Liza shrugged. "My mom gave it to me to check my hair." Then Liza smiled and looked at Howie. "Besides, you never know when you might need one to catch Count Dracula."

"Well, here's your big chance," Melody said. "He just came into the cafeteria."

The four kids watched as Mr. Drake whisked over to the lunch counter. He poured a tall glass full of the pink lemonade and popped in a straw. In one giant slurp, he sucked the glass dry.

"Wow! He must have been really thirsty," Eddie said.

"That's because he didn't drink enough today," Howie whispered. "Wish me luck." Without another word, Howie hid the mirror in the palm of his hand and walked over to Mr. Drake.

"Hi, Mr. Drake," Howie said. "I was wondering if I could talk to you."

Mr. Drake smiled, showing his pointy eyeteeth. "Certainly," he said. But when Howie flashed the mirror at him, the counselor swooped away. "I cannot talk now," Mr. Drake called over his shoulder. "I really must fly!"

Before Howie had a chance to check Mr. Drake's reflection, the school counselor fled the cafeteria.

"Rats," Howie snapped when he plopped down at his table. "I almost had him."

"It doesn't matter," Melody whispered.

"Of course it does . . ." Howie started to say, but then he noticed his friends. They were pale and staring past him to the back of the lunchroom.

"What's wrong?" Howie turned around and looked. Beside the back door was a glass panel. Two sixth-grade girls were combing their hair in front of it. Howie saw their reflection.

"Did Mr. Drake walk past that mirror?" Howie asked.

Melody, Liza, and Eddie nodded slowly. Howie took a deep breath and asked, "Did he have a reflection?"

Without saying a word, Melody, Liza, and Eddie slowly shook their heads.

9

Vampire Huey

"What happened to Huey?" Liza asked when they got back into their classroom. Huey's desk was empty.

Mrs. Jeepers flashed her green eyes toward Liza. "Poor Huey did not feel well. He went home sick."

"Sick to death," Howie whispered before Mrs. Jeepers silenced him with a stare and started the class on a science experiment.

The four kids didn't get a chance to talk about Huey or Mr. Drake until after school. They met under the oak tree. "Huey's a goner," Howie told them. "He's Count Dracula's newest vampire."

"I'm scared," Liza whimpered.

Eddie dropped his backpack on the

ground. "I don't believe this hogwash. There's got to be a perfectly logical reason for all this."

"What about his reflection?" Howie said with his hands on his hips.

Melody twisted one of her black braids around her finger. "I've been thinking about that. Maybe our eyes were playing tricks on us, or we just couldn't see Counselor Drake's reflection because of those sixth-graders."

"Don't you see?" Howie told them. "Mr. Drake is Dracula and Huey's his latest victim. That's why he went home sick."

Eddie shook his head. "Huey probably just ate too much for lunch."

"Then let's go to his house and find out for ourselves," Howie dared them, wrapping his red scarf tightly around his neck. "If he's not a vampire, then you have nothing to worry about."

"I'm not worried," Eddie said, grabbing his backpack. "Let's go."

In five minutes the kids were ringing Huey's doorbell. "I don't like this," Liza whined. "He might get mad and bite us on the neck."

Eddie laughed. "Huey eats a lot, but he hardly ever bites third-graders." Eddie stopped laughing as the door slowly squeaked open. A tall, pale woman opened the door and stared past the kids.

"Um, excuse us," Howie said softly. "We were worried about Huey. May we see him?"

The pale woman shook her head slowly. "No," she said in a dead-sounding voice. "No one can see him."

"We . . ." Howie started to say. But the woman closed the door without even looking at him.

"She really acted weird." Liza shivered as they walked away from Huey's house.

"She acted like a vampire," Howie said. "I bet Huey already bit her!"

"Yikes!" Liza said, grabbing her neck. "I'm sleeping with a turtleneck on tonight."

"Don't worry," Howie told his friends. "I know how to save Bailey City from Count Dracula."

10

Magic Dust

Eddie rolled his eyes and jumped up to catch the lowest branch of the oak tree. It was early the next morning after Huey went home sick. The playground was completely empty except for Melody, Liza, Eddie, and Howie.

"There's nothing wrong with Mr. Drake that a day at the beach couldn't solve," Eddie told his friends. "That dude just needs a suntan."

Liza pushed her blond hair out of her eyes and shook her head. "No, there's something very mysterious about him. I really think he *is* Dracula."

"We could put him on a show called *Lifestyles of the Pale and Weird*, but that doesn't make him Dracula," Melody giggled.

Liza shivered. "You heard him say he was always thirsty. What if he starts sucking the blood of everyone in Bailey City?"

Eddie dropped down from the branch and looked at Liza. "Being thirsty doesn't make him a bloodsucker."

Melody nodded. "It doesn't prove a single thing."

"Maybe not," Howie said. "But this will." He held up a crinkled bag of his favorite snack, garlic potato chips.

"Those chips are disgusting," Eddie muttered. "They taste like dead warthogs."

"I like them," Howie reminded Eddie, "but that doesn't matter. What matters is that they have garlic. Vampires can't stand garlic!"

"That's right," Liza said. "If he really is Dracula, the king of the vampires, then these will send him packing."

Howie smiled. "And Bailey Elementary will be safe once again. I'm going to sneak these into Counselor Drake's office before school starts. Then we'll know by lunchtime if Mr. Drake is or isn't Dracula."

Eddie had to race to catch up with Howie, grabbing his arm to stop his friend. "You can't just pile a bunch of chips on his desk."

"Besides," Melody reminded him, "Mrs. Jeepers doesn't allow us to bring junk food into the building."

Howie nodded. "Smart thinking."

Eddie grinned. "Well, someone around here needs to keep thinking."

"Piles of potato chips are too obvious," Howie said, ignoring Eddie. Howie stood very still, then he snapped his fingers. Before anyone could stop him, Howie dropped his bag of garlic chips and stomped on it.

"Why did you do that?" Liza gasped.

Howie picked up the crumpled potato chip bag and pulled open a corner. He sprinkled finely crushed chips into his hand. "That is just what we need. Mr. Drake will never notice this. Dust. Magic garlic dust."

"You better use some of that dust on yourself," Eddie snapped, "because you're under a magic spell . . . a dumbbell spell."

"Don't be so sure," Liza interrupted. "Look!"

She pointed to the street where Counselor Drake was darting from shadow to shadow. The collar of his black coat was pulled up high, covering his face. He swooped to the door of Bailey Elementary just as Ben walked up the steps. The four kids watched as Ben and Counselor Drake disappeared inside the building.

"I think Mr. Drake just ordered break-fast," Liza said with a shiver.

"Not if I have anything to do with it," Howie said bravely. Then he followed Counselor Drake and Ben into the deserted halls of Bailey Elementary School.

11

The Chips Are Down

Eddie, Liza, and Melody followed Howie, their footsteps echoing eerily in the early morning quiet. Most of the classrooms were still dark and only a few teachers could be heard writing assignments on the chalkboards. Every once in a while the foursome passed another student, but Counselor Drake and Ben were nowhere to be seen.

"Where did they go?" Liza whispered.

"Where do most vampires take their victims?" Howie hissed.

"The cafeteria?" Eddie joked.

Howie glared at his friend before speaking. "No, to their caves. Their vampire lairs."

"There aren't any caves in Bailey City," Melody said.

"Mr. Drake's lair is the nurse's office," Howie said before stomping toward the office. Melody, Eddie, and Liza had to hurry to keep up with him.

Liza jogged up next to Howie. "You can't just go barging into a vampire's lair and throw garlic dust at him."

"Do you have any better ideas?" Howie asked. Liza shook her head, and Howie went into the principal's office alone. The nurse's office was a small room inside the main office.

"Don't worry." Melody patted Liza on the shoulder. "Howie will be fine."

"Of course he will," Eddie snapped, pushing past the two girls. "Especially since I'm going to help him escape from Counselor Drake."

"But you don't believe he's Count Dracula," Melody pointed out.

Eddie turned to face his friends. "But I know everything there is to know about getting out of trouble. And Howie's going to need me after he throws a bunch of stinking crumbs in school. Besides, Mr. Drake is one strange cookie."

Liza gasped. "So you *do* believe Howie."

Eddie shrugged. "I believe Howie needs help."

Melody and Liza looked at each other, before looking back to Eddie. "Then we're going with you," they told him.

The three friends found Howie tiptoeing past Principal Davis' empty desk. Very slowly the four moved toward the nurse's office, careful not to make a sound. Howie gripped the potato chip bag.

Closer and closer they came, until they were just inches away. Liza dug her fingernails into Melody's arm, and Howie pulled his red scarf up around his neck as they stepped into the dimly lit office.

"Oh, no," Liza gasped. "We're too late!"

12

Fly Home

A very pale Ben sat in a corner of the room, staring into space. Melody rushed over to him. "Are you okay?"

Ben shook his head. "I feel terrible. I'm going home."

"What's wrong?" Liza sounded as if she didn't really want to hear the answer.

Ben opened his mouth, but just then something big and dark swooped into the room. Liza screamed and Eddie ducked under the nurse's desk. Howie jumped back, scattering potato chip crumbs over everything, including Mr. Drake.

"Ahh-choo!" Mr. Drake sneezed and dabbed his nose with a silk handkerchief. "What are you students doing here?" he asked.

Howie gulped and Liza closed her eyes.

But Melody said in a strong voice, "We came to help Ben."

"Help me?" Ben said with a sniffle. "I just have a cold."

"A cold?" Howie asked. "Are you sure?"

Ben nodded. "There's something going around. I'm sure I'll be fine by this evening. Now, all I want to do is sleep. But it was nice of you to worry about me."

"See?" Counselor Drake smiled so big his pointy teeth showed. "You have nothing to worry about. Nothing at all."

Melody, Liza, Eddie, and Howie left the office without a word. But out in the hall, Eddie was the first to speak. "Was it my imagination or was Ben actually nice?"

Liza hugged her arms. "I didn't know that was possible."

"Anything's possible when you have Mr. Dracula for a counselor," Howie said.

"Sorry, kids," Principal Davis said as he walked up beside them. "Mr. Drake

68

won't be your counselor after today. Too many things in Bailey City stir up his allergies. Seems like everybody's sneezing lately. Counselor Drake is flying home tomorrow night."

"Fly?" Liza gulped.

"That's the only way to travel," Mr. Drake said from behind them. The kids turned to see Mr. Drake and Ben walking out of the principal's office. Ben was even paler than before.

"Remember, no fighting," Mr. Drake told them before whisking down the hall. Principal Davis patted Ben on the shoulder and went into his office.

"No more fighting for me," Ben said with a smile. "See you guys later." Ben walked to the fourth-grade room. Liza, Eddie, Melody, and Howie stared after him.

"I don't believe it," Melody said. "Ben really is friendly."

"It took a dead-looking guy with bad teeth to make Ben a nice guy," Eddie said.

"I bet Huey and his mom have a cold just like Ben," Liza told her friends. "Mr. Drake is nice after all."

Howie sneezed and wrapped his red scarf around his neck. "Nice for Count Dracula," he whispered to himself.

Debbie Dadey and Marcia Thornton Jones have fun writing stories together. When they both worked at an elementary school in Lexington, Kentucky, Debbie was the school librarian and Marcia was a teacher. During their lunch break in the school cafeteria, they came up with the idea of the Bailey School kids.

Recently Debbie and her family moved to Plano, Texas. Marcia and her husband still live in Kentucky where she continues to teach. How do these authors still write together? They talk on the phone and use computers and fax machines!

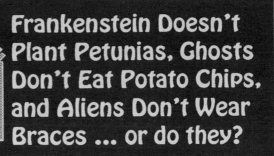